Little Gorilla

Story and Pictures by RUTH BORNSTEIN

ISBN 0-590-12086-7

Copyright © 1976 by Ruth Bornstein. Spanish translation copyright © 1978, 1994 by Scholastic Inc. All rights reserved. Published by Scholastic Inc. MARIPOSA is a trademark of Scholastic Inc.

15 14 13 12 11 10 9 8 7   8 9/9 0/0

Little Gorilla

For Harry, a nice father gorilla

Once there was a little gorilla, and everybody loved him.

His mother loved him.

His father loved him.

His grandma and grandpa, and his aunts and uncles loved him.

Even when he was only one day old,
everybody loved Little Gorilla.

Pink Butterfly flying through the forest,

Green Parrot in his tree,
and Red Monkey in her tree,
all loved Little Gorilla.

Even Big Boa Constrictor thought Little Gorilla was nice.

Young Elephant, and Old Elephant too, came to see him.

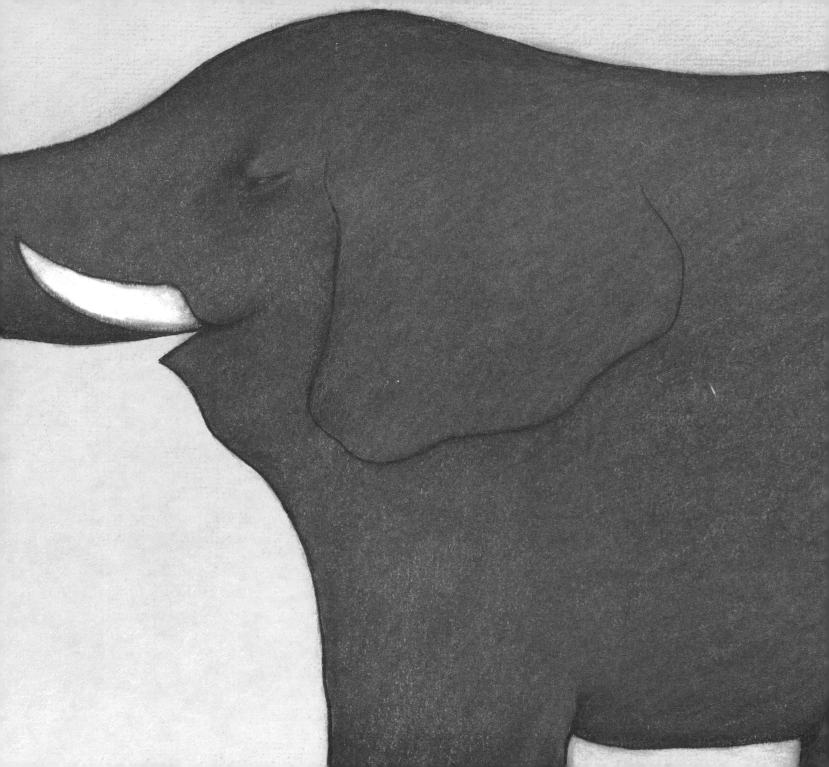

Lion roared his loudest roar for him.

Even Old Hippo took him wherever he wanted to go, because she loved Little Gorilla.

Just about everybody in the great green forest
loved Little Gorilla! Then one day something happened . . .

Little Gorilla began to grow

and Grow

and Grow

and GROW   And one day,

Little Gorilla was BIG!

And everybody came,

and everybody sang

"Happy Birthday Little Gorilla!"

And everybody still loved him.